The Adventures of Pintsize Plasma

Race at Bedbug Park

by Jean Horst

Copyright © 2014 by Jean Horst

First Edition – January 2014

Make a Dash for the Trash

Pintsize Plasma
www.pintsizeplasma.com
Bed Bug Buffet

ISBN

978-1-4602-2640-7 (Hardcover)
978-1-4602-2641-4 (Paperback)
978-1-4602-2642-1 (eBook)

Produced by:

FriesenPress

Suite 300 – 852 Fort Street
Victoria, BC, Canada V8W 1H8

www.friesenpress.com

Distributed to the trade by The Ingram Book Company

The Adventures of Pintsize Plasma

Race at Bedbug Park

"Mom, help, my toe is stuck! I'll be late for the race," cried Pintsize Plasma.

Mom raced over to rescue Pintsize Plasma's tiny foot from a thread in the mattress.

"I thought I'd never get free!" he cried and quickly swiped away a tear. Pintsize didn't want to look like a baby. He snatched his nightcap from his head and pulled his fuzzy slippers from his tiny feet.

"Quick, Mom! We need to get to the race. Fast! I want that prize."

"I know, baby. You practiced all summer and you are ready to show everyone what you can do," Mom encouraged.

"You have an hour before the race starts. Let's get you something to eat to give you more energy," she said. "Come on, baby. Climb up to the top of Abby's bed and take a sip from Mr Brown, Abby's dog."

"I'm not going up there. Abby scares me. She tried to swat me the last time I got near her," said Pintsize. "I must have tickled her leg while trying to get closer to Mr Brown. Her hands are faster than Dyno Mite's feet!"

"Don't worry your little head. Abby will be sleep-ing soundly," Mom told him. "Today was her first day at school. She won't even notice you if you don't get too close. And after the race, as a treat, we are going to have a picnic at Bedbug Park. I will have some of your favorite treats set up on the food table.

"Now off you go—a tiny sip from Mr. Brown will get your six little legs speeding across the finish line, baby."

"You better be right." Pintsize crept very cautiously onto the bed, hoping not to disturb Abby. Pintsize thought Abby looked so cute and peaceful when she was sleeping. He would never try to hurt her. As long as Mr. Brown didn't wake up, then Abby would stay asleep too. Pintsize crawled carefully onto Mr. Brown's back foot, took the teensiest sip and rushed back across the bed toward his mom and out of danger.

"Mommy, p-l-e-a-s-e, promise me you won't call me 'baby' in front of my friends," Pintsize begged as he grabbed his hat and ran out the door on his way to the race at Bedbug Park.

"Step up, contestants! Listen for the starter's gun," the starter cried in his loud, booming voice. "Any false starts will eliminate that contestant."

Pintsize got on his mark, ready to take off at the crack of the gun.

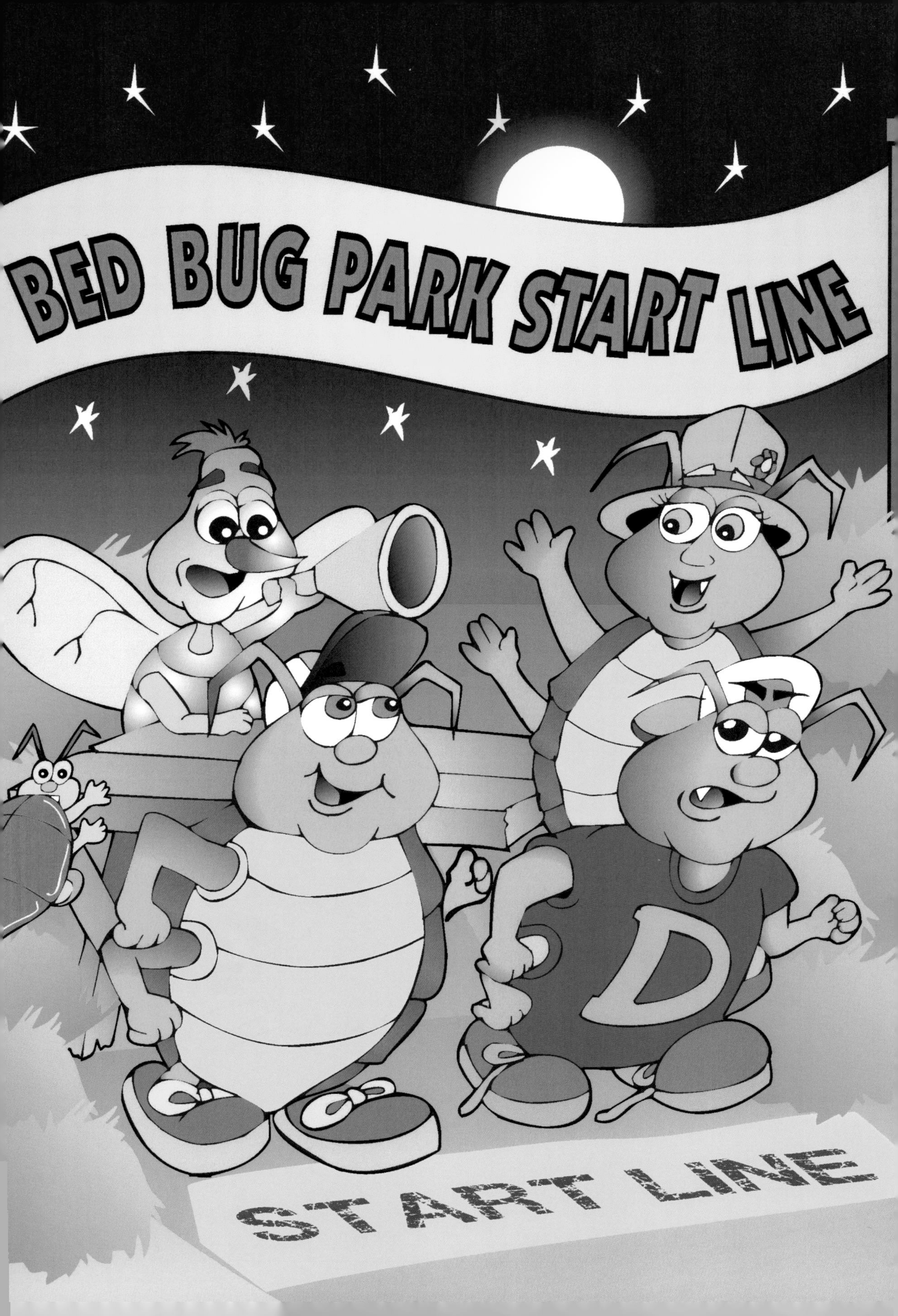
BED BUG PARK START LINE
D
START LINE

"Nice running shoes," screamed Cindy Mite from the sidelines.

"Watch me win this race!" Pintsize yelled back. "These shoes will propel me over the finish line like a rocket."

Pintsize really wanted the prize. He'd been running from one end of the mattress to the other all summer to get ready for the race. But he was secretly worried that Cindy's brother, Dyno Mite, would beat him to the finish. Dyno was bulging with muscles and he was much stronger than Pintsize. Dyno Mite was the favorite to win this race.

"I'll see you at the picnic after you win," Cindy Mite yelled back with a smile and a wave. The gun boomed and she watched Pintsize take the lead. Cindy thought her brother's head was getting too big. She hoped that Pintsize would beat Dyno to the finish line.

Pintsize burst from the starting block and surged past the other runners. Only Dyno Mite was in front of him and Pintsize gave every bit of energy he had in him in an attempt to over-take his opponent. He had the finish line banner in sight when suddenly he found himself tumbling over Dyno and sliding along the ground.

* * *

"Great job, kid!" yelled Pintsize Plasma's dad, reaching down to help his son up from his fall. "Are you OK?" He wiped a drop of blood from his son's scraped nose.

"Dad! Who won?" Pintsize didn't care about his nose. "I tripped at the finish line and fell into the banner."

"You sure did. And that is why you won . . . by a nose," Dad laughed. "If you hadn't tripped, Hemo Globulin would have beaten you. But your nose was just ahead of his foot when you went down," Dad chuckled.

"If you're OK, let's get over to Bedbug Park before all the seats are taken. I'm starving. But I bet you aren't hungry, kiddo," Mr. Plasma teased.

"I'm waiting for the prize ceremony," Pintsize said. "I'm too excited to eat. Dad, do you mean that Dyno Mite didn't even come in second?"

"No, Dyno tripped and got tangled up in those green shoe laces he was so proud of. He didn't even finish," Dad assured his son. "In fact, he may still be trying to disentangle himself!"

"Before the picnic begins," announced Mr. Arthropod, the Master of Ceremonies, "let me introduce you to the winner of the ski trip to Skin Flake Hill. Pintsize Plasma, will you please come up to the winners' circle and take a bow," he yelled out.

Pintsize jumped up and ran to the front of the room.

"Good job, young man. You deserve this," Mr. Arthropod said, handing Pintsize the winner's cup and the envelope with the tickets for the ski trip. "What have you got to say for yourself?"

"Wow, I can't believe I actually won," he said, grinning from ear to ear. "Thanks, Mom and Dad, for letting me stay out all night to practice. I had a few close calls when my human family rolled over in bed. But I survived. It all worked out. I can't wait to go skiing!"

"I have one more shout out," Pintsize continued. "I want to thank Dyno Mite, whose big muscles inspired me to work harder. And thanks, Dyno, for tripping up so I could beat you."

When the applause and laughter died down, Pintsize called out, "Now that the race is over, I have my appetite back. LET'S EAT!"

Pintsize spied many of his favorite treats on the buffet table, and his mouth began to water. There was red boil stew, plasma parfait, and platelet pie with hemoglobin dip. And to drink there was a yummy, vital juices cocktail. For a special treat he noticed that his mom had made her famous blood-red jelly and glucose cookies.

As he carried his overloaded plate back to his table, Pintsize heard Dyno Mite yell at him.

"Pintsize, hey dude, amazing performance. Hope to see you at Skin Flake Hill. You better start practicing, buddy. I'm challenging you to a race down the slopes!"

"That's a challenge I'm glad to accept," Pintsize yelled back. "Maybe you'll have better luck staying upright on skis," he laughed.

"Ladybugs and Gentlebugs, can I have your attention for one last important message,"
Cindy Mite shouted from the podium as the party was starting to break up.

She continued, "As much as I loved seeing my brother tied up in his laces and brought back down to earth by my superhero, Pintsize Plasma, I don't want anyone else tripping on something that has been left lying around on the ground. So as your event co-ordinator, I'm asking everyone to sing along with me as I recite a little ditty that I made up while I was waiting for my turn at the podium," she said. "Jump in and join me if you feel the urge. The number is called:

MAKE A DASH FOR THE TRASH

Make a dash for the trash,
Let's keep Dyno on his feet,
Make a dash for the trash,
Keep our world tidy and neat,
Make a dash for the trash,
After every yummy treat,
Make a dash for the trash,
To keep bruises off Dyno's seat.

Howls of laughter rocked the park. When the noise died down, Cindy added,

"My brother has a sense of humor. I know he'll be happy we are doing something to help mother-nature."

By the way, "I have temporarily placed a home-made sign over the trash can."

"Thanks for coming out and supporting your community. And please, as your leave, 'make a dash for the trash', with all your garbage."

Back home, Mom tucked Pintsize into his crack near the headboard. "Baby, here's a new quilt I weaved for you from the softest baby hair and toe lint. I knew you'd win," she whispered, leaning down to give him a kiss.

"The sun is almost up. It's time for you to get some sleep."

"Mom, thanks for not calling me 'baby' in front of everybody," Pintsize called as Mom scurried over to her own mattress crack.

"No problem, honey," she smiled. "But you are still my little baby."

"I don't know what I'd do without you, sweetheart. And it looks like I have a little competition now that Cindy calls you, her **superhero**," she teased and noticed her son's cheeks turn red.

The race was over and at last Pintsize could sleep all day without worrying about Abby rolling over and squishing him.

As the last stars lost their twinkle and the sun started to rise in the eastern sky, Pintsize closed his eyes. He thought about the game he and Hemo liked to play. They took turns jumping over Sam, Abby's brother, without getting swatted. And soon our little bedbug drifted off to sleep, dreaming of the great adventures he would have tomorrow.

ABOUT THE STORY
(The Adventures of Pintsize Plasma)

by
Jean Horst

A warm, gentle, breeze rippled through the new, soft-green, tender leaves of the giant maple that covered most of the front yard of this old summer place. The kids and I had named it the Lakehouse. It is an evening in early June. I rocked in my chair on the front porch, listening to the tree frogs and crickets and the sounds of early evening. The warmth of these soft breezes enveloped me as they held all the dreams of a fun-filled summer being re-ignited.

I had just come from checking on my grandkids. Moments earlier, I had ushered them to their rooms after finishing our hotdogs and lemonade. Today's hot, sunny afternoon had been spent on the beach playing in the soft sand and crystal clear water by the shores of Lake Huron in the small Scottish town of Kincardine.

This summer place is far enough removed from any large metropolis so that the winters become long, lonely, blustery acts of isolation and endurance, while the summers bring bursts of bustling vacationers. These expectant sojourners carry with them the excitement of sunny, warm and lazy weekends filled with boating, swimming, sandcastles and barefoot walks along the beach enjoying the warm sand and soft surf.

24

Occasionally the town hosts a summer festival in the park or a fishing derby at the harbor. Evenings are set aside for barbeques, boisterous partiers and Scottish festivals filled with music and the lonesome wale and squeal of bagpipes.

Every Saturday night at 8:00, in the summer, the pipe bands parade down the main street, and tourists and townspeople as well as the occasional, newly wedded, bride and groom, fall in behind to march with the band.

At sunset, a lone piper climbs to the top of the lighthouse with his bagpipes and serenades the sun until it falls behind the deep blue water of Lake Huron.

Sometimes, on a Friday afternoon, I will pick the kids up after school, and with mom and dad's blessing, we drive the two hours up to the lake for the weekend. This was the first excursion of the year for the three of us. So I was shocked to find that my normally energetic grandkids had already climbed into their beds with their jammies on and had fallen sound asleep.

It brought to mind the old saying, "Sleep tight. Don't let the bed bugs bite."

Now, rocking on the porch again, and listening to what reminded me of a babbling brook as the silver leaves of the poplars whispered and rustled, I drifted into a semi-sleep and began thinking about what it would be like to be a bedbug.

And thus was born, "The Adventures of Pintsize Plasma: Race at Bedbug Park."

Abby and her brother listened intently as I read the story to them a few weeks later. Observing how much fun they had seeing these funny characters come to life, I thought other children might want to read this tale as well.

Below is a picture of Abby, dreaming of Mr. Brown and Pintsize and looking like a taste of summer, that early June night.

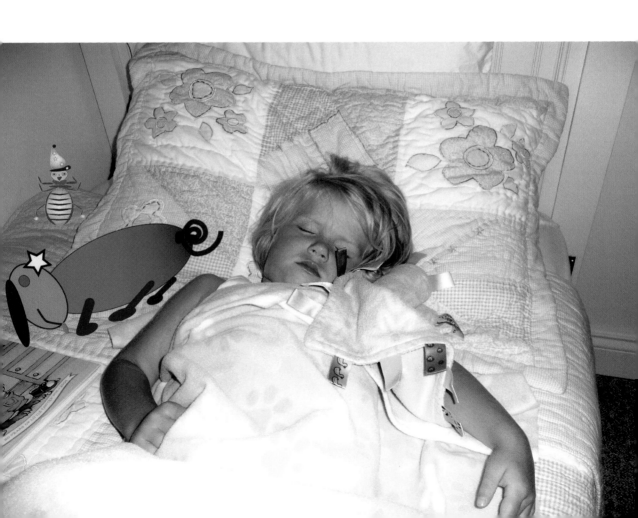

CPSIA information can be obtained
at www.ICGtesting.com
Printed in the USA
LVIC06n2329040314
375666LV00004BB/18